UNDER A SUNFLOWER MOON

Cherokee Stories and Poems

JACKIE KRAFT, M.S.

QUILL
HAWK
PUBLISHING

Printed in the United States of America.

For more information, or to book an event, contact:
asunflower.moon@gmail.com
(http://www.underasunflowermoon.com)

Jacket design by Virginia McKevitt
Photo Credits – Wikipedia Commons and Jackie Kraft, M.S.

ISBN: 979-8-9875646-7-7 (paperback)
ISBN: 979-8-9875646-8-4 (hardback)

Contents

Dedication 3

Preface: Three Corn Necklaces 5

1 Greeting the Sun 7

2 Poems from the Trail 11

Grandmother Trueshot 11

Drumming 13

Making Good Trail Soup 14

The Trail of Cold Tears 1838-1839 16

Corn Woman 18

14 Clans, Now Seven 21

The Trail of Real Names 24

Angels 26

Sadness 27

Medicine Bundle on the Trail 29

Council House 31

Kindling the Sacred Fire Under Three Stars 34

Medicine Bundle at Trail's End 38

Honoring Red Mud 39

3 Poems of Humbug on the Trail 40

Mother Was a Star Woman 40

More Ice 42

How to Bury a Star Woman 43

Soul's Journey 46

Hold My Hand. Sweet Jesus 48

Difference 49

Buffalo Waltz 50

New Inventory of a Medicine Bundle 53

Mistress of the Red Mud 55

My Sorry Soul 57

4 Creation and Clans 58

5 Forget What You Know About Manatowa 61

6 Grandmother Trueshot's Teachings 65

Those who Cried out for Return   65
Finding East   68
Rage and Raccoon Stew   69
Sing the Snakes to Winter Sleep   71
Once in Silence We Went Where Eagles Rest   73
Rain Making   77
Rose Quartz Harvest   80
7 Uncle Scoot   82
8 Sally's Poems   86
Blue Corn Harvest 7/08/14   86
Hidden Garden for Shy Deer   88
October Day   90
Gathering Corn Pollen For My Medicine Bag   93
Sweet Smell of Tobacco   95
Deer Season: How to Tan Hide   97
More Than the Sum   99
Brave Warrior   102
When Adam Braided Eve's Hair   103
Gift of the Spider   104
Paul 4/2015   107
Dance   109
Belonging   111
Turtle Wisdom   112
Downstream from Politics   114
Forgive Me, as I Forgive Others   115
The Clan of the Sunflower, the Humble   116
Ladybug, and the Moon
Appendix 1   121
Appendix 2   123
Appendix 3   126
About the Author   127
Acknowledgments   128

Dedication

This book is dedicated to my family, teachers, and friends. Thank you for all your encouragement.

Three Corn Necklaces

Preface
Three Corn Necklaces

Mrs. Tiftley was nearing ninety when she asked my grandmother if she could give me a gift. We were drinking tea. I was almost seven that summer of 1950. It was in the evening under a Sunflower Moon.

"I've had these three corn necklaces since I was a child," said Mrs. Tiftley. Gently she set her teacup on the saucer. Her trembling hands reached for the little box on my grandmother's outdoor table. She rested both hands on the lace tablecloth, then opened the lid and drew out three corn necklaces.

"They are strung on cotton thread, but each is tied with deer skin at the ends."

I saw two corn necklaces were yellow. One was deep red. Leather knots tied at the ends.

"What is Yellow? What is Red?" she asked, smiling at me.

I shrugged my shoulders, puzzled.

"East is red; heaven is yellow," my grandmother Cora answered. They both nodded. Grandmother asked then, "Who made these? Was it your mother, Many Stars?"

"Yes, *Elise,* Many Stars, from her own garden in Georgia."

"To help you remember where we come from."

"Yes, near Keetoowah Mound. Near the beautiful River of No Return. To help me remember our Deer Clan."

"We are also Deer Clan, aren't we, Grandma?"

"Yes, Sally, but my mother Eliza Ann and father Perry died when I was 14, so I don't know much."

"Try them on," said Mrs. Tiftley sipping tea. "First the red and then the two yellow. The two yellow also stand for the sun and the moon. Both are important to the Cherokee."

I put them around my neck one at a time. Grandmother passed peach jam and a plate of blue corn muffins.

"Cora, let Sally come to me each morning after breakfast. I will teach her the ways of the Deer Clan."

"I'll do that," answered my grandmother smiling. "Could you also tell her the story of how we came to have blue corn for a harvest?" She tenderly put another blue corn muffin on my plate. She smiled again.

CHAPTER 1

Greeting the Sun

Before the sun rose today over the Cherokee Oklahoma Reservation, the birds began to sing. The full Sunflower Moon lingered in the night sky waiting to greet the sun.

My grandmother tied a small feather cloak of white feathers around my shoulders and took me by the hand. "It is your birthday. You are seven years old today."

We walked in moonlight up the hill to the Widow Tiftley's back alley. Sunchokes grew in borders all around her garden. Her kitchen light was on, and we could smell breakfast cooking.

"Knock on her screen door, Sally," said Grandmother. I saw Mrs. Tiftley standing inside the door waiting for my knock. "*Osiyo.* Hello. Sally came to greet the sun and start her knowledge of our ways. She knows a little already, but you are the real teacher."

Mrs. Tiftley opened the screen door slowly, "*Osiyo.* Hello. Come down these stairs to the garden of our three sisters. In the middle is my mound. We will stand there and watch the sunrise. Welcome. You are right on time."

Mrs. Tiftley led us to the center of her garden. We climbed the small mound and faced the eastern sky becoming pink. Gradually in silence we watched the sun rise from its dark sleep.

Mrs. Tiftley said, "I've prepared a table on the south side for breakfast with the three sisters, as well as some wild potatoes. Cora, stay until Red-Tailed Hawk flies overhead. Eat with us. I will bring Sally home after her lessons."

Grandmother nodded and asked, "Who are the three sisters, Sally?'

This answer I knew. "One sister is squash like pumpkins, or crooked-necked squash. Next are beans. The last sister is corn, dark red corn or yellow."

The sky was becoming yellow and lighter pink.

"And, Sally, what are wild potatoes?" Mrs. Tiftley took me by the hand and led us to her table as we talked.

"Can they be sweet potatoes?" I asked. I wasn't sure.

"Sometimes, if we don't have sunchokes."

"What are sunchokes?' I asked.

Grandmother smiled as she sat down to a table set with a freshly ironed red tablecloth and four napkins. "Look around you. Do you see all the Sunflowers?"

I nodded. They were everywhere and as tall as me. Some sunflowers were even taller. Their green leaves were heart-shaped. Their yellow flowers were turning to face the warm sunshine. I sat down on the chair Mrs. Tiftley showed me.

She said, "Sometimes if we don't have sunchokes, we cook sweet potatoes. Chokes are the roots of our wild sunflowers that grew everywhere long ago in our swamps near the beautiful River of No Return where once we camped and had organized towns. Out here in Oklahoma on the reservation, we can't always find the wild sunflowers."

"Once our clans walked a cold trail to Oklahoma," said Grandmother. "Sunflowers grew everywhere in abundance and very interesting wild walking birds feasted among them under the yellow sunflowers."

Mrs. Tiftley's youngest daughter, Mattie, brought food out

for us to eat. She stayed.

"My uncles could catch the little birds with their bare hands," said Grandmother.

"My uncles used blow darts to hunt birds," answered Mrs. Tiftley. "They found hollow rivercane for the blowpipes. They also made their own darts. They would find a locust tree and make darts. Then they would attach down from a thistle or find soft feathers from a chick."

"The little birds were so good to eat!" Grandma had told me this before.

I said, "Did they fly like eagles?"

"No," answered Mrs. Tiftley's daughter as she smiled.

"But they could fly up a bit if they were frightened." Mrs. Tiftley put food on my plate, and then passed each dish to Grandmother.

"Nowadays a schoolteacher, like me, will say they are called 'Northern Bob Whites,' but we say *'tis a gwa'* in our language."

The sun was partly up giving us a very pale shade of golden pink. It was the beginning of a late summer blue sky. Near the tree line, three deer grazed on willow branches. A family of four raccoons gathered a harvest of new strawberries. They washed their food in the creek.

"Today, Sally, we eat corn, beans, and squash in honor of our three sisters who liked to be together. They thrive in a garden of love just as we do. It's not your usual breakfast. And we eat sunchoke potatoes to honor the season of sunflowers."

"*Ogali Agali*. Hello, Sunshine," said Grandma.

"Look," I said, "What bird is that up there making circles high about us?"

A large red-tailed bird circled overhead in the blue morning sky.

"A Protector," said Mrs. Tiftley's daughter.

"A Protector, sacred to the Cherokee," said Grandmother. "Come to see you learn our ways. Rare in these parts, but welcome. A bringer of good fortune."

"A particularly good omen for Sally. A sacred Protector. The Red-tailed Hawk --- She brings you strength, power, and courage. Gifts for your birthday. We are Cherokee. We look for omens. Your

Cherokee name is *Tsalagi Ana Yunwiya*."

"You can have many names; some are kept secret for protection," said Grandmother. "Yes, your American name is Hawkins. You are also *Ani ga du wagi* or *Kitawah* People in our language."

"My name is Sally Jacqueline Ann Hawkins." I took a bite of corn, beans, and squash. What a wonderful food combination. I loved the flavour, and I liked my name. It was a combination I cherished. "I am Cherokee. One of my Cherokee names is Little Humbug. I have another Cherokee name, but it is secret. We greet the sun like a Sunflower."

Grandma and Mrs. Tiftley's daughter nodded at me. Mrs.Tiftley chewed her food and smiled at me. "Today we will talk about Cherokee things. I will tell you of my Great Grandmother Trueshot, who drove a wagon out here on the Trail of Tears, but tonight we will dance under a Sunflower Moon."

A Sunflower Moon Rising

CHAPTER 2

Poems from the Trail

Grandmother Trueshot

My Grandmother packed her wagon
Before the sun came up.
There was just enough room
Some of us grandchildren
And my baby brother could ride with her.
I sat at the back of the covered wagon
And watched the single file
Of aunts and uncles follow us behind.
Grandmother set the pace

Under a Sunflower Moon

And called for our breaks.
At her feet on a quilt of red and white cotton
Was a cast iron bucket
Of small burning oak coals that
We used to start our campfires.
She didn't hunt, but if all the men
In our clan died, she would.
She taught me how to start a fire,
To skin rabbits, squirrels, raccoons, and deer.
She taught me how to save their hide,
How to plant a garden.
How to sew,
How to use everything we found.
She taught me how to dress a chicken,
And make a stew.
How to draw the rain
And sing the snakes to sleep.
She taught me how to milk a cow,
And drive a team of horses pulling her wagon.
But mostly she let me ride
When I was tired of walking.
She let me warm my feet by her smoldering bucket.
She told me old stories as we traveled the sad trail
Of how the rabbit got long ears,
Of how the raccoon got his mask,
Of how the white-tailed deer got his antlers.
She let me warm my heart with her words.
She was my best and oldest friend.

A Deer Resting

Drumming

I have a precious little kettle
I cover with a deer skin
When I don't cook,
I use the kettle as a drum.
When I don't cook,
I put the deer hide skintight over the kettle.
I tie it down with sinew.
There is fresh water in the bottom
Of the kettle to remind us
Of the great flood.
(Some say Noah's flood.)
I brought it on the trail west.
When we dance,
When we stomp,
Grandmother Trueshot drums
Like a storm is coming.

13

Trail Soup

Making Good Trail Soup

When you are on the trail
And on a day of rest
Carefully take off the Deer Skin cover
From your kettle.
Fold and put away.
Greet the Sun.
Say a blessing for all the directions.
Fill the kettle with one bucket of water.
If the soup is for our Deer clan,
Make a fire of White Oak logs.
(If the soup is for all Cherokee,
Build a fire using seven logs,
One wood sacred to each clan.
Then bring more kettles.)
Add four onions, maybe more,
Add one or two heads of cabbage

14

Jackie Kraft

Torn in pieces,
Five carrots, six fish caught fresh,
Nine or ten potatoes.
Then put in squash, beans, and corn.
Add tomatoes and bear grease,
If you have some,
And two pinches of salt.
Let it cook all day long.
Thank everything you put into the kettle.
Thank the fire.
Thank the logs.
Thank the spoon and bowls you use.
Thank the Creator,
Whose name we don't say out loud.
Pray the fish forgive us for catching
And killing them to the nourishment of our body.
Thank them for such abundance in the rivers.
Let the men and children eat first.
Moms, Grandmas, and other women eat last.
The four women, who cooked, then eat.
I am one.
First, I remember the Seven Sisters.
Some call them the Seven Brothers.
Some say they are the Pleiades,
Where the sky people came down
From in the heavens.
Who really knows?
I just say a prayer of thanks to them all.
I fill my belly with food.
Finally, we all rest and be thankful.

Yellow Corn is a Symbol of the Sun and the Moon.

The Trail of Cold Tears 1838-1839

It's cold.
No one in my tribe cares.
We bite gray snow in big gulps.
We eat frost.
We go from good homes full of food
To no place warm.
Good-bye to tall trees.
Good-bye to well-tended gardens.
Good-bye to large rivers.
Good-bye to Turtle Island
And sacred White Oak Trees.
Good-bye to sweet owls of long, dark nights.
Good-bye shy deer, my sisters.
Good-bye Horse-shoe Bend.
Good-bye to good luck.
Some of my tribe stay to hide in dark caves.

Jackie Kraft

They fear bears less than guns and new laws.
No one sings.
Our hearts break in two parts.
One part stays in Georgia and the east.
More snow comes to cover our steps.
We walk in long lines
With harsh winds in our face.
Some cry as they walk in sad lines
With cold ice-flakes in our faces.
Some drive wagons, but horses die.
Drivers die.
We starve.
Our children die.
Our old warriors die.
Our old whispering grandmothers die.
We bury each beside the River of No Return.
On each dead breast we plant the three sisters
To keep them company.
We plant one corn kernel, one squash seed, one bean,
Just in case we come this way again
On the trail of cold tears.

The Three Sisters, Corn, Beans, and Squash

Corn Woman

The old corn woman
Was milling corn.
She held the dried corn in two hands
Then wrung the seeds off
Into the basket between her knees.
She asked me why I came.
"I seek truth why my tribe must leave?"
"In shadows and in sunshine,
The truth is all the same," she said.
"What can I believe?"
She answered me.
"You may never know the truth.
Except to say some crave gold so much
They will kill you all and do evil.
The old corn woman put her task aside.
"Where we live is where there is gold.
Here, take these corn necklaces to wear,
I made them just for you.
When you wear them,
You will remember how
We plant, dry, and mill our corn.
I said, "Are you going, or
Will you hide and stay?"
"Fat Pie and Slow Bear come early tomorrow
To pack my wagon.
Here take this basket of seed corn, also.
It is full of love, hope, and life.
On the trail you can
Trade the seeds for thoughts more valuable than gold."
She stood up and got her black cast iron skillet
From the nail on the post.
She put the skillet on the iron spider
Above the low fire.
"Get the bear grease.
Let's make popcorn."

18

When the grease was hot enough,
She threw in dried corn kernels.
We listened to the corn pop,
And considered our fate.
I said, "Tomorrow you can bring your loaded
Wagon to my place.
Bring your cows and chickens.
We can leave together.
Will your sons go,
Or will they stay and hide?"
"We don't know yet."
The corn stopped popping.
The old corn women
Threw in a small handful of salt,
And a dollop of cow butter.
She stirred the popcorn.
"Come," she said, "Let's sit on my front porch.
It's time to sing the snakes to their winter sleep.
We'll eat first."
I said, "Who will gather feathers for us now?"
She answered, "I hear Oklahoma has
Buffalo, Rattlesnakes and Eagles,
So we will be fine.
We will be grandmothers there."
We ate in silence, then I said, "There is nothing better
Than bear grease and popcorn."
She nodded. She began to sing the snakes to winter sleep.
I sang along.
Finally, I stood to leave.
She put seed corn into another cloth bag for me.
She said, "When planted, water Hope with your tears.
Catch rain in your open mouth.
Forget your fears,
Because Heaven cries with you.
Plant with love.
Pray for healing.
Think of good from up above.
Forgive everyone and everything.

Under a Sunflower Moon

Especially gold seekers who steal our land.
Enjoy Life.
Teach your daughters how to plant.
How to harvest Hope.
How to sing.
Tomorrow I'll be right behind you
On the trail."

Kituwa Mound

Jackie Kraft

14 Clans, Now Seven

We were once fourteen clans.
Now we are only seven clans.
Father carried our medicine bundle
As we walk the trail of cold tears.
Ice is good.
It is now our friend.
It helps to think in slow, hard ways.
We are numb.
We let go of our homes on green hills.
Ice helps us forget our blue lakes of big fish.
We forget much food.
We forget warm sleep in soft beds.
Ice is our new friend come to teach us
How to keep up with change.
We were once 14 clans.
Now we are seven very sad clans.
Here's who we are:

I

We are *A ni wa ya*, the Wolf Clan,
Who absorbed the Panther Clan,
Once separate from us.
Now they are in our clan too.
Our color is red, the color of rust.
We bring the seeds and wood
Of the Hickory tree.

II

We are *A ni go da ge wi,* the Wild Potato Clan.
Our color is green,
The color of new tobacco plants.
We bring seeds and wood of the Birch tree.

III

We are *A ni wo di*, the Paint Clan.

Under a Sunflower Moon

Our color is white, and we are secretive.
We are Corn People.
We bring seeds and wood of the Locust tree.

IV

We are *A ni sa ho ni*, the Blue Stone Clan.
Our color is blue like Blue Holly
Used for medicine.
We bring seeds and wood of the Ash tree.

V

We are *A ni gi lo hi*, or the Long Hair,
Or sometimes called the Twisters Clan,
And sometimes called the Strangers.
We go by many names.
Our color is yellow.
We have white feather robes.
We bring seeds and wood of the Beech tree.

VI

We are *A ni tsi s qua*, the Small Bird Clan.
Or color is purple.
We use blow guns.
Air is sacred to us.
We bring seeds and wood of the Maple Tree.

VII

And we are my Clan,
A ni a ha wi,
The Clan of Shy Deer.
Our color is soft brown,
Like the Earth we roam.
In the new land we will be given
A flag of purple with yellow stars.
We bring seeds and wood
Of the White Oak tree,
So sacred to my clan.
Used to kindle the sacred fire.

VIII

All clans honor the seven directions,
The four helpers of wind, earth, stone, and fire.
Many of us die.
We give our dead back to Mother Earth
Along with a kernel of Corn.
A seed of Squash,
One little Bean.
We walk on to Oklahoma
With tired feet
On ice trails
Made of fresh tears.

Snow on the Trail

The Trail of Real Names

I don't know the names of all
The Cherokee who walked the trails west.
I know who in our clan
Walked with Grandma.
I know who hunted,
And who helped cook.
I know who set up camp
Beside us each evening
And ate with us.
I know who greeted the morning sun
And prayed with us.
I know who we buried.
I know who made it all the way.
I know who carried the sacred bundle,
Who walked before me,
And who cried as they followed.

Jackie Kraft

I know who huddled together to keep us
All warm when the snowstorms came.
I know who started this whole misery
And who was born into this nightmare.
I know who kept our hope going
And who got their hearts broken.
I know who was there to be counted
At the end of the trail for real people.

Angels

In desperation I cried for help.
A gentle breeze from many wings
Surrounded me and swept me close.
Angels whispered my name
As sunlight shone through their words.
Softly they said, "Remember us?"
Now, when I shiver
Through strong storms,
Along the Trail of Cold Tears.
I feel the fierce winds of mighty wings
Fighting for wretched, lonely me,
Knowing the pure power of love
From my friends, the steadfast Angels,
Fearless, I lean now
To the center of their strength.
Surrounded, I cling to love
From steadfast Angels.

Sadness

With a cap of snowflakes upon her head,
And a breath of ice upon her lips,
Sadness came swirling in
On the winter wind to visit us.
Her dark eyes sparkled
As we listened to the
News of our father's sudden death.
Sadness laughed
At my little brother's tears.
She touched my mother's head
Causing a silver hair to grow.
With a hateful finger
She marked a wrinkle on my brow.
We turned our backs on her,
But she held up memories for us to see.
We closed our ears
To her constant, cruel murmurings,
But she gripped us by the shoulders

Under a Sunflower Moon

And stole into our minds
Tearing at our thoughts
Until we could ignore Sadness no longer.
The funeral delighted her
As she hovered near the flowers,
We tried to lose her,
But she slipped her sinister arms
Around our waists one by one
And beckoned us to draw nearer.
And as a last, final hurt
Sadness did an icy, unkind dance
On our father's grave.
We loathe her presence, fear her closeness,
And despise her horrid way of always
Slinking up to find us.
We watch her from a distance
With our faces half-turned
As she tries to eavesdrop.
Daily we encourage her to go,
But we know
Sadness is here to stay.

Jackie Kraft

Medicine Bundle on the Trail

I now carry the Medicine Bundle.
Yes, I, a child, I carry it.
For my family.
For what few of us are left in our Deer Clan.
How will we know Deer Medicine?
If I don't take it with us?
Who will teach us?
With every step I walk on this death march
My turtle shells rattle around at my knees.
I feel the skin of a first deer kill
That wraps my bundle of sacred medicine.
I feel the shape of two deer antlers

Under a Sunflower Moon

(One each from two separate kills.
I was not there on the kills.)
They press against my chest for good luck.
Some people ride in our covered wagons
With all we could gather for the trip.
I hear the distant sounds of real people
As they walk with turtle shells rattling at their knees.
We few are the carriers of the Medicine Bundles.
The turtles knew their sacrifice.
I know mine now.
I learn by carrying the bundle.
I will carry it the long way to a new home,
And all through my life,
Wherever I go through my life,
I will carry it in my arms
And in my heart and soul.
And I will find new medicine
To make our people thrive
In a new land for us.
The new place is not called Turtle Island.
It's called the Cherokee Reservation ---
If we can believe the promise
That it is land set aside for us for all time.
Our Tribe, we who survive, will bring
Our knowledge of the Universe.
Together we will teach the sacred directions of
Up, Down, Center,
And East, South, North, and West.
Once I get there, I, Mary Stars,
I just want to know how far
I will have to walk
To get salt and bear grease?

Chief John Ross

Council House

Our old Council place
Had seven sides, one for each clan.
Seven is sacred to the Cherokee.
Our Chief is John Ross.
We will build a new Council House
There will be one place for each
Of our seven clans
Which were once 14.
And one side, one empty place
For whom I cannot say,
Maybe for invisible Bears, or maybe Sky People.
In the middle will be the sacred fire
Made of seven kinds of wood.

The *Kituwi,* The Square, will be nearby.
Who will be the first to kindle the new fire?
No one tells me yet.
We never talk to outsiders
About what is sacred to us.
We never talk to outsiders about
Or Sky People and their cloud ships.
I'm changing that some
Because I have been told
"Now is the time.
Here will be the place."
I will tell the truth of how they visited
My little brother and me all our lives.
Some of the Deer Clan
Are messengers as I am.
They will begin to talk as I will.
By an unspoken river
We will now build our new Council House.
We will talk of things sacred to those
Who warm themselves by our fire light.
We will share our Cherokee knowledge.
We will speak of Eagles, Eagle Feathers,
Fire, Smoke, Suns, Moons,
Corn, tobacco, raccoons, and panthers
Every seventh year, Red Tail Hawks,
Ketoowah Night Hawks,
Rattlesnakes,
Our seven directions
Of North, South, East, West,
Up, Down and Center.
Quartz crystals kept in an Arc,
Little gray people who teach us all.
Three Elders who keep the fires,
(Cho Ta Auh Ne Le Eh)
Turtle Island,
The Four Mothers Society,
And how a Priest is chosen in his childhood
To use herbs and crystals.

And how the *(Ani Kutani)* Priestly Clan was destroyed
For reasons not discussed openly.
We might not talk about people
Who became invisible like the bear,
Or disappeared completely,
But we can talk openly about
(*Manitawa Yow*a) The Supreme Being,
Whom only a priest or medicine man
Can say his name
Because he or she created the sun, the earth,
The moon, the stars,
And us, the real people,
The Cherokee Nation.
We will talk openly about
How to dance and to learn
Under a Sunflower Moon.

A Sunflower Moon

Camp Fire

Kindling the Sacred Fire
Under Three Stars

I
We bring 7 logs to the top
Of the mound, one from each clan.
Sometimes we bring 14
In remembrance, in honor, of what once
Was the sacred fire for 14 clans.

II
Flags of our clans are a new thing,
Created after we come to Oklahoma.
Flags, one for each clan,
Are brought and staked
Around the center fire.
We collect near our clan flag.
I honor life, death

And rebirth as I stand near.
The old fire is extinguished, but who will
Kindle the new fire?
Still, no one tells me.

III

I am a friend of the Wolf Clan
And of their tree, the Hickory.
They are the friends of the panther,
And the spirit of the sacred fire.
Blood red is their flag with three white stars.
Our leaders come from this clan.

IV

I am a friend of the Small Birds Clan.
Maple is their sacred tree.
Purple is their sacred color.
They revere air and wind and blow guns.
Eagles are sacred souls and Red-tailed Hawks
Are scared birds to their clan.
Their flag is blue with red stars.

V

I am a friend of the Wild Potato Clan.
They honor their tree, the Birch.
They honor tobacco
And all the plants that grow on Mother Earth.
Their friends are the earth, the raccoons,
And the bear that is sometimes invisible.
Their flag is yellow with green stars.

VI

I am a friend of the Long-Hair Clan,
Sometimes called the Twisters
Because of the twisting ways they walk.
They adopt the Strangers and the Orphans
Who blow in with the wind.
Yellow is their sacred color

Under a Sunflower Moon

Like the sun's golden breath.
Their flag is black with white stars.
The Beech tree is theirs to love.

VII

I am a friend of the secretive corn people,
Called the Clan of the Red Paint
With their copper red dirt paint
And their Locust trees.
Their color is pure white,
But their flag is black with red stars.
They love air.

VIII

Because my clan is the Deer Clan,
I am a friend of messengers, finders, and Nighthawks.
Our color is brown, but our flag is the purple
Of an early summer evening
With three white stars.
Our tree is the sacred White Oak.
We also love swans and buffalo.
Our clan brings messages
Of peace and the good life.

IX

I am a friend of the Blue Holly Clan
Who revere purification.
Their tree is the mighty Ash
And their friends are the wildcat,
The bear and the panther.
Their color is blue and their flag
Is Iris blue with white stars.

X

Here is how we got the first sacred fire long ago:
We were living in a cave high in the mountains
When the rains came.
The water collected and surrounded us.

We had no way to get food or stay warm.
From our cave opening we watched the storms
And the lightning set fire to trees below us
Sticking out of the water.
We watched the brave red spiders gather fire
In their little baskets on their backs
And swim to us with that fire.

XI

We marveled at the way God provided us
With that gift from many humble spiders.
When the water went down, we noticed the trees
And the wood they each provided.
Each clan chose
Their wood from a special tree for kindling.
When we light our fires, we remember the sacrifice
The little red spiders made to bring the fire
In their tiny baskets to us in the caves.

XII

We cherish all the gifts of the spiders,
Just as we cherish the sacred gifts
Of the turtles who swam with spiders.
The turtles brought us food to eat.
They carried the food in their stomachs.
They carried corn, squash, and beans
For us to eat as well as plant.

Flag of the Cherokee Nation

Medicine Bundle at Trail's End

My bundle is not a burden.
I carry a bundle
Full of my totems.
It is not easy to sit with Eagles,
Or hunt with bears,
Or run with panthers and buffalo,
Or go on a Warpath.
I'll leave that to my brave brothers
Who eat Raccoon Stew,
And sleep with snakes in the wilderness.
My bundle is full of sacred objects.
They protect my clan and give me hope
For a new home on red mud banks
By a clear river
In new land named Oklahoma.

Honoring Red Mud

The best red mud is right by the river bank
When a late rain has made it soft.
Mosquitoes are not my brother.
They are not my sisters.
They are not one with my spirit.
I will not let them suck
My Cherokee blood
Because I have a plan.
First, I will smell the honorable,
Dripping red, wet mud.
Then will I smear red mud
Over my whole body,
Over my face and scalp,
Through my toes and up
Over my naked body.
I will say, "Aye-Yi, swoosh and more good,
To little biting bugs,
But you will not ruin my
Cherokee night
Under a Sunflower Moon.

A Campfire on the Trail

CHAPTER 3

Poems of Humbug on the Trail

Mother Was a Star Woman

Mother was a star woman.
She slept under a blanket of fireflies.
She said, "Night comes
When you can see
Three stars in the evening sky.
The night is always your friend.
Watch for the fireflies to arrive.
They try to be shooting stars.
Watch for the big bear and the little bear.
In the daylight, they are invisible.
At night they guard the fierce raccoon

And help the night hawks and the warriors
Find their way."
We make a campfire and watch for stars.
Where will we bury Mama
When she dies?
Once she told us, "The time to pick apples
And look for lucky white feathers
Is in the daylight,
But the time to learn things
About the world from your elders
Is at midnight.
Elders will teach what Cherokee need to know.
Wait for knowledge to come.
Learn at midnight
The night is always your friend.
The stars will each tell you a story."
I said, "What is your favorite story?"
My brother and I gathered close to her robes.
"My favorite is how, AYVDAQUALOSGI TSI S QUA,
The Thunderbird,
Saved his seven daughters.
That giant Thunderbird took them
To heaven in his mighty wings.
They all became stars.
Time went by.
The seven sisters come back in a cluster
To shine on us at night
After we make a harvest.
They stay all winter to show us
There is hope in the darkest days.
Finally, in the spring,
When it is time for us to plant again,
They leave.
Sometimes when I feel ill,
The seven sister stars, *Shu Shu Khem*
Come down from heaven
To comfort me.
They hold our hands when we die."

41

MORE ICE

Ice is good,
It is a friend.
It helps us think on this trail
In slow, hard ways.
We are now numb to love.
We forget our homes on green hills.
We forget blue rivers and lakes,
Big fish, much food,
We forget warmth and
How we slept in soft beds.
We forget dreams.
Ice is our new friend
Come to teach us
How to keep up with change.
How to swallow our silent screams.
How to forget love.
How to forget hope.
How our heart hurts when our mother,
Many Stars,
Our sweet Star Woman, dies.

Jackie Kraft

How to Bury a Star Woman

I
It won't be easy.
There will be many frozen tears.
I will tear my clothes in big rips of pain.
I will scream agony in the black night.
But I will bring the shovel from the wagon
And dig the first hole.
I will melt my frozen tears
With my hot, wild screams.
We will find a good hill
Beside the River of No Return.
We will wait for three stars to come.

II
Then we will watch for the Pleiades,
The seven sisters rising,
The Shu Shu Khem,

Under a Sunflower Moon

In the eastern night sky
To join our Deer Clan as we mourn.
Those sisters will watch me bury Mama
And watch me plant acorns
From White Oaks on her breast.
Our clan brought the acorns to mark
The trail of cold clan death.
If we ever come back this way,
We will look for a cluster of tall, grown
White Oak Trees, sacred to our clan.
We will plant corn, beans, and squash,
Those three sisters who will
Wake the soul of our mother
In the springtime with their roots.
Mother was a Star Woman.
I buried her with all my love.

III
Yes, I, a child,
Dug the first small hole.
My little brother, Strong Hawk, sat nearby
Under his blanket and watched.
He held my medicine bundle,
The bundle that holds
One rose quartz crystal,
(Probably I don't deserve
To have this sacred crystal,
But I'm keeping it anyway.)
Two deer antlers, for double good luck,
And small leaf of tobacco
Gathered at dawn near Turtle Island long ago.

IV
Our Deer Clan now comes closer
To keep us warm.
My little brother and I are shivering.
We huddled together to keep warm
As we slept on her grave that night,

Just for tonight under Grandma's fur robe.
In the morning we said a farewell chant
Through our frozen tears.
We sprinkled corn pollen on her grave
It felt empty to push on without her.

V

In the spring we thought of her
And reminded ourselves
Her soul will rise to heaven.
She will thank the Seven Sisters, or brothers,
For holding her hand in theirs
And watching over her grave
Under the snow and ice.
We will remember her around all
Our new campfires through the years,
Or when we see three stars in the night sky,
Or see the cluster of the Pleiades rising.
We will remember her stories.

VI

Often, we are told by the elders
She will give back her own blessing
To the Universe for giving her life,
For letting her be a Star Woman,
For letting her be of our Deer Clan,
For letting her know the
Wonders of this world,
For letting her be our lovely Star Mother
And for being born a Cherokee.
For making us, my little brother,
Strong Hawk,
And me, Humble Bug, be born Cherokee.

Three Sisters

Soul's Journey

Some wonder why the Soul even
Bothers to enter a human body.
Soul could have lived in a rock or a tree.
Yet she chose to be a live person.
She is a mystery and comes from God
On a journey
In search of the meaning of life.
Everything and everyone she meets
On her life's journey

Jackie Kraft

Brings her lessons
On beauty,
Kindness, faith,
Justice, friendship,
Hope, honor,
Victory, Death,
Humor, Pain, Fear, Courage,
Truth, the sun, the moon, the stars,
Trust, Love, and Community.
She needs something from our world,
A knowledge of harmony
To take back with her to heaven.
In the beginning of her journey
She came down bringing life
To the innermost parts
Of a real person, a Cherokee.
She opened her eyes seeking the light.
She asked, "What is the true nature
Of this beautiful, but cruel Universe?"
She saw this truth:
The Lord is a generous God.
He forgives our sins.
He waits for us to learn.
He creates everything to exist
With its opposite.
Did my Mother, the Star Woman,
Feel her journey to earth
Was worth it?
Did her soul go back to visit
All the Cherokee places she had lived?
Did she let go of anger?
Did her soul go back to our old beliefs,
Or did she stay a Christian?
Did the journey make her soul free?
When she met God face-to-face,
Did she ask, "What is the answer?"

Hold My Hand, Sweet Jesus

Hold my hand, Sweet Jesus,
As I wave good-bye to Momma.
Wipe my tears away.
Walk beside me in this cold.
Warm my heart with your presence.
Hold my hand through
Rain, Snow, Wind, and Ice.
Lead me when I stumble.
Tell me how to turn my other cheek.
Tell me how to forgive.
Hold my hand now
As I wave good-bye to Mama.
Wipe my frozen tears.
Hold my hand now
As I wave good-bye to love.

Jackie Kraft

Difference

Do you know the difference between
One who sees magic,
And one who does magic?
There is a difference between
One who sees ghosts,
And one who is a ghost.
There is a difference between
One who sees beauty
And one who creates art.
There is a difference between
One who communes with Sky People,
And one who is the real sky person come to commune
With us, the real people, The Cherokee, here on Earth.
Do you know who you are?
Do you know your place in the Universe?
Can you see and feel the difference?

The Seven Sisters

A Herd of Buffalo

BUFFALO WALTZ

Now we are here in Oklahoma.
We will build new homes,
But not so warm,
Not so great,
Not so full of food.
We see the Buffalo wallows
And ask when, when, when,
When will the animals travel
Through this land to roll again in dust?
Now we will wear our Buffalo masks
And do a dance for Buffalo
To come our way.
"Come," We sing, "Roll in the red dust,
Crush the bugs that bite you.
Feel the warmth of the earth.
Come, run across the empty land,

50

Jackie Kraft

Feel the free wind rush your mighty faces.
Sorry, big brothers and sisters,
We must shoot arrows, fire guns, stab you,
Hit you with our sticks and clubs.
You will die, that we may live.
Sorry,
Sorry, Sorry.
Your blood is on us all.
You now become us.
Your flesh becomes our flesh.
Your soul is wrapped up in us,
The Deer Clan,
As we feast on you.
When we can't find Deer to kill,
We must eat you.
Sorry, Sorry, Sorry.
We see the world now
Through your small, sad eyes.
We feel full.
We feel grateful,
But, still, there is sadness everywhere.
We will leave a gift of salt
Where you died for us.
I will keep your tail bone
In my medicine bundle
For good luck.
And I think in my heart ---
This ear, your ear, will I tan.
This ear, your ear, will I save.
It will be one buffalo ear
To place in my sacred medicine bundle
For when I need to call you.
I'll take it out of the bundle
When we are hungry;
I will hold your little ear so gently,
So very gently,
So tenderly in both my Deer Clan hands,
And I shall pray for your forgiveness

Under a Sunflower Moon

One more time and wipe away tears
As I sing to you
A new "come-to-me" song.
You will like my little Cherokee waltzing song.
It will be my gift to you before you die.
You will love me for sweetly calling you
To your death with my waltz.
I promise.

Some in hidden caves

Jackie Kraft

Rose Quartz

New Inventory of a Medicine Bundle

Bear Grease
Salt
Rose Quartz Crystal
Two deer antlers for luck
Tail bone of a first-kill Buffalo
Ear of a mighty first-kill Buffalo
Piece of red flannel
One copper coin,
One silver coin
Twig, leaf, and acorn
Of a sacred White Oak Tree
One Raccoon foot,
Caught by my Uncle Fat Pie,
One Golden Eagle feather
From my grandfather called Spotted Frog,

Under a Sunflower Moon

One Bald Eagle feather
From a Real Person I will not name,
Four Bear Claws
Seven Tobacco Leaves
One swan feather
Beans, Corn kernels, Squash seeds
Corn pollen gathered at dawn.
One clump of dried-out red mud
From the River of No Return
For good luck
Under a Sunflower moon.

The Verdigris River, Oklahoma

Mistress of the Red Mud

I watch for the moon rise
And look for three stars.
I feel powerful as I make a crown
Of bean and squash blossoms for my hair.
I roll in red mud tonight
Until I feel Cherokee again.
I watch the sun go down.
Did Eve ever feel this good?
Did she ever get to roll naked in red mud?
Did she bathe herself in clear streams?
Before God braided her hair with roses
In the Garden of Eden
And gave her to Adam?
I thank my Creator
For making me smarter
Than mosquitos
In search of fresh blood.
I like to sit naked on the red banks
Of my new river in Oklahoma

Under a Sunflower Moon

Under the sunflowers.
I watch for white-tailed deer.
Did Eve ever want to howl all night
At the new moon and the stars?
Did she ever want to dance?
Did she ever feel in charge?
Was she ever mistress of the red mud?

Jackie Kraft

Chief Cunne Shote

My Sorry Soul

In my soul is a poem deeply hidden,
Wanting to cry out.
Shimmering words
My heart has kept close
That if let loose would fly
Like straight arrows
Into the sky.
My heart and sorry soul
Are bound up in secrets never whispered,
Not allowed,
Golden, shimmering,
Iridescent feelings of love
Wanting to be heard,
Wanting,
Waiting,
To be moaned to the heavens.

CHAPTER 4

Creation and Clans

Mrs. Tiftley told the story of our beginnings. "In our words we have no name for cave, but once we lived inside Mother Earth. We lived high in the mountains of what is now North Carolina."

She said, "It rained for many days and nights until the water came up the side of our mountain - almost to our opening in Mother Earth. We had no food."

"Now we have lots of food to eat." I watched her give me strawberries on my yellow plate. It was late September, early in the morning. We sat in her garden again at her lovely table.

"I love all the food you give me," I said.

Mrs. Tiftley smiled. "When we were in the cave we had some food, but after a long while, it began to run out. We had no food, and we were very hungry. Turtles swam to us. They came to us in threes and fours so we could live. Each turtle brought a gift in her belly. Some big turtles brought three gifts for us to plant when the water went down.

"We saved the gifts to use later; some little turtles we cooked and ate. We made turtle soup. Afterwards, we made turtle rattles with their shells to remember them by. What do you think the gifts they brought were, Sally?"

"Do you mean some kind of food in their bellies?"

"Yes. Like food."

"Well, could it be the foods they ate?"

"Yes. They brought seeds. Most turtles brought corn. Some brought beans. They all brought squash. We saved all the seeds and later planted them together."

"Then you called them your sisters, the three sisters to us."

"Yes." Mrs. Tiftley took a sip of her tea and continued.

"In that time the sky was gray with endless rain. In that rainy time the Creator whose name we don't say aloud, gave us the sacred fire. It came by lightning and hit certain trees. At first the brave little water spiders brought fire to us in baskets on their backs. We got the fire idea from them.

58

"But how could a spider have a basket and carry fire?"

"I just don't know," she replied. "Brave people went out in the rain and rescued the burning logs of tree before the rain could put out the fire. We gathered other sticks and logs, dried them out in our cave. We could make a cooking fire in our caves. We made rattles of the turtle shells. Finally, the sky was blue again. The rain quit, and the water began to go down."

Grandma and my cousins were there with us that morning. "We all crawled out of Mother Earth and sat in the mud. It was wonderful to feel the warm sunshine on our faces. It was good to go outside our cave again." She took strawberries for her plate.

Mrs. Tiftley said, "We chose our tree for a home at first. We lived in the shade of our tree as the earth dried out. We chose our animals for a totem, and we named our clans. We brought the sacred fire from our cave, the three sisters to plant when the mud dried, and the rattles to tie around our knees. We celebrated our survival."

Grandma opened her bag. "Here are my rattles. I wear them around my knees when I stomp. We did not wear them in the old days. But now we are starting Pow Wows. Sally, at our next Pow Wow, I will put turtle rattles around your knees. My shells have the three sisters in them. Some women don't have turtle shells, so they will use tin cans filled with pebbles to make noise. It's a joyful noise."

"We were so happy to see the sun that we got up early every morning from then on to greet her. We planted the three sisters. The corn grew tall. The beans climbed and grew up the cornstalks. The squash vines grew across the ground to choke out the weeds. We had plenty again to eat. We called Mother Earth our Turtle Island because once we and the turtles were surrounded by the water."

"The rain was a blessing."

"And so was the lighting, the thunder and the turtles."

"The Creator chose us to eat turtles. Do you know the fiercest animal there is, the raccoon? We must be fierce like the raccoon even in our hunger, fear, and sorrow. He eats turtles, too."

"We called ourselves the principal people, the *shay ro ki*." Grandmother finished her tea.

But sometimes we call ourselves the *chay ro ki to wi,* the principal people of the first, most prime place, the Turtle Mountain, and the keepers of the sacred fires." Mrs. Tiftley finished her tea. She leaned toward me, "For years we have honored our secrets. We told outsiders nothing of our secret ways, but now is the time, and here is the place to tell all."

"Well, not all. We will tell a few of all the secrets," nodded Grandma. Mrs. Tiftley smiled at both of us.

A Cherokee Woman

The Racoon so Fierce

CHAPTER 5

Forget What You Know About Manatowa

It was raining. Mrs.Tiftley welcomed me into her warm kitchen.

"We might not be able to greet the sun this morning, Sally, because there is just too much rain and too many clouds."

"The rain is a blessing." said her daughter Mattie as she hung up my sweater. She handed me a towel to dry my face and hands and hair. "We don't' get enough of it here in Oklahoma."

"Come. Eat and drink something," Mrs. Tiftley smiled and pulled out a chair for me at her kitchen table. Each place was set with red and yellow Fiesta dishes.

"What will I learn today?"

Mrs. Tiftley passed me some warm blue corn muffins and some strawberries. "I might tell you how we got our blue corn. It's not something that the Cherokee had native where we lived originally."

There was a loud knock on the back door. The cat ran for cover. Uncle Scoot came in.

"May I join you for breakfast?" He shook off the rain and hung up his jacket.

We all made room for him at the table. Mattie poured him a cup of coffee in a Fiesta cup. The aroma fresh hot coffee filled my nose. "Thank you, Mattie. Did you make the blue corn muffins?"

"Yes. I ground the flour from the blue corn myself early this morning. Here is some peach jam to go on it."

Mrs. Tiftley said, "You can help us tell Sally how we came by blue corn."

Uncle Scoot looked at me as he carefully spread the jam on his muffin. "Well, Sally, first we will have to tell you about The Valley of the Warm Vapors."

"And the Ouashita Mountains," added Mattie. She filled my glass with milk, "And the Hot Springs."

"And how our ancestors came there to that sacred place for a visit a long time ago." Mrs. Tiftley sipped her coffee and settled into her storytelling position. "I should start with the rain, I guess."

Mrs. Tiftley leaned forward and turned toward me smiling. "The rain is truly a blessing and long ago in what we now call the state of Arkansas there was a lot of rain. No one knows exactly when the first Native Americans came into the area of the Ouashiita Mountains. Some say it was 8,000 to 10,000 years ago. The big rains may have come later, about 4000 years ago, it is thought."

Uncle Scoot continued the story.

"But whoever came there, they first noticed a beautiful valley lush from all the rain. Once there were swans and buffalo that came to drink in the lakes and the streams. After the rain quit, it was possible to see mist rising from the ground. The raccoon came at night to hunt fruits and vegetables.

"When the first people walked around and among the mist, it felt warm on their faces and bodies. Sore places began to heal. Open wounds no longer festered but grew over with new flesh. Everyone felt their aches and pains go away."

Mrs. Tiftley said, "On drier days people would sit by warm springs up and down the area. Some springs were very hot, but that was only more comforting. People began to feel that the creator had made a place where everyone could find healing and respite. White-tailed deer were prevalent in this region and still are to this very day. They knew the value of this place."

We all nodded at Mrs. Tiftley's words. We ate some strawberries.

She continued, "Word spread as everyone came and returned to their villages feeling healed and renewed. People talked of the Valley of the Vapors. It and the hot springs became a sacred, holy place to gather. Now, we know the hot springs are full of healing minerals."

"All tribes regarded it as a neutral place where The Great Spirit lived and breathed. The smoking waters were the breath of the Great Spirit. It was miraculous," said Uncle Scoot. "Eventually the Quapaw, the Caddo, the Osage, and the Tunica settled in areas nearby. One day *Cheera,* one of our ancestors and his wounded brother *Couey,* came to the Valley of the Vapors for healing. Everyone was welcome. Anger and revenge stayed home. Everyone brought gifts to give to others who were there from many tribes."

"They brought Tobacco leaves. They traded for rose quartz crystal rocks, gold nuggets and bears claws," Mrs. Tiftley nodded at us.

"One man brought his young sick son from a very long way out west. They were Hopi dressed differently than us, and they wore their hair within what we call bangs. His name was Harmony. Well, he said it in sign language. I don't know his name in his language." Uncle Scoot continued.

"Harmony explained that their hairstyle signified that he and his tribe watched for sky people, and especially the *Blue Kachina* to come down from the sky. He had blue corn kernels to trade. He explained the Creator gave his tribe the last kind of corn kernels. They were blue. We know the creator gave us, the Cherokee, yellow and red kernels on big cobs. His tribe received the small blue corn that grew in rows on tiny cobs. It still makes good corn flour. Other tribes got bigger kinds of yellow and white corn on larger ears."

Mattie said, "*Couey* and *Cheera* brought blue kernels home to us, and some of our people have had it ever since to plant and harvest."

"It makes good muffins," I took a bite. "Will you teach me how to grind the flour and bake them? I want to visit Hot Springs sometime. Have you been there?"

Hot Springs, Arkansas

A Black Panther in His Favorite Tree

CHAPTER 6

Grandmother Trueshot's Teachings

Those who Cried out for Return

It took 300 years before the Israelites
Returned from slavery in Egypt
To their promised land.
God gave them the land of milk and honey.
What was their evidence?
In a court of law, years later,
After the Jewish Holocaust,
The Bible was used
As a document to prove their case.

Under a Sunflower Moon

Once our Cherokee land was hills and streams,
An abundance of everything we needed.
We did not have a promise from God
That the land was ours.
Did we really need one?
I wonder?
We knew the truth.
No one really owns the land.
It belongs to God and Mother Earth.
We always found a good place to set up camp and
Then moved on whenever we wanted to move.
There were those who cried out
On the Trail of Tears for our return.
The Eagles circled in the sky.
The Panthers slept in Hickory trees.
The Red-tailed Hawks perched in White oak trees.
Snakes slept under rocks in the mountains.
The Deer wept silently as we left our homes.
Why were we leaving?
I saw my mother's footsteps falter on the trail.
I saw her tears.
Some drove wagons and cried.
Some went on horseback and cried.
Some rode or walked and cried.
Mostly some died.
We buried many.
One day after brave warriors
Such as Morning Breeze
And Falling Meat
Died on the trail,
Grandmother Trueshot said,
"So many of our men are dying,
We must teach everyone everything,
Or our ways of doing will die away, too.
Not everyone knows how to be a deerslayer.
Not everyone knows how to tan deer hide.
Not everyone knows how to sing
The rattlesnakes and copperheads to sleep.

Jackie Kraft

Not everyone knows how to make a medicine bundle.
Not everyone knows the reasons we gather corn pollen or tobacco,
Or why we honor sacred directions.
Not everyone knows how in silence
To talk sign language
When it is time to gather
Golden Eagle feathers,
Not everyone knows the next steps
Of how to clean, save
And prepare their black and white feathers
In silence for our tribal needs."
She paused.
Not everyone can be a man and a warrior.
She looked me, a little girl, in the eye.
"Some girls are very young,
But each can learn as well as boys."
Grandmother Trueshot took up the task.

Sunrise in Oklahoma

Finding East

"Make your home and your heart face East.
Speak Cherokee to your children.
Teach them sign language.
Remember everything that is sacred
To our tribe and the Deer Clan.
Be humble and respectful to others,
To all plants and animals.
Help others remember our heritage.
Help others remember their clans.
Keep the rising sun in your heart.
Even on the darkest day,
Even on the darkest night,
Even in the hardest times,
Even when your fears are greatest,
Even when you have lost everything.
Keep light, hope, and healing in your heart.
Keep a prayer on your lips.
Everyone must now be a silent warrior.
True East is what you seek."
It was Grandmother Trueshot's honor to teach.

A Cherokee Woven Basket

Rage and Raccoon Stew

We, our tribe, doesn't go on the warpath anymore.
Not since the Civil War of 1861.
Some Cherokee fought on the Yankee side.
Some Cherokee fought for the Confederates.
Some of us, my family, had brothers on both sides.
How rage ripped us apart!
After that war,
We were left with even less.
We don't make raccoon stew anymore.
We made it for the warriors to eat
Before they went on the Warpath.
Why?

Under a Sunflower Moon

Because the raccoon is the fiercest animal there is.
Raccoon Stew is made like Trail Soup,
But made in Silence.
There is no laughter.
The only meat is the raccoon.
Soup is made in silent prayer for our tribal men.
The silent prayer is for the fierce soul of the raccoon
To join and guide each Warrior
On his raging path
To Victory.
We women don't eat Racoon Stew.
We rest and keep praying.

Sing the Snakes to Winter Sleep

After the last of the Sunflower moons,
After the last of the harvest days,
When the air begins to feel much cooler,
And the daylight seems much shorter,
It is time to think of Deer Season
And the blessings we say for the kills.
It is time to sit and rock on the front porches
With a blanket on your knees to keep you warm.
It is time to sing the snakes to sleep.
"I start by whispering prayers to all creatures
Who sleep with their eyes wide open,"
Said Grandmother Trueshot.

71

Under a Sunflower Moon

"I ask them if they are looking for some place warm?
Perhaps under a nice big rock to spend the winter?"
It's dark under a rock. It's dark and fine in a nice hole.
Seven days I sing blessings on those who must go to sleep.
Slither away, I hum.
Find your favorite place to go.
I'll watch the world while you rest.
Then, at the end of my rocking chair time,
I take a nice nap.
In silence, I arise and speak in sign language.
It is time for me to get the Deerslayers
And make ready to go into the hills.
It's time for me in silence to send for one
Or two Eagle Killers
And four Eagle feather gatherers.
It is time for snakes to sleep and
Time for us all to bless the silent kill.
Time to dress meat and time to tan hides.
Time to build new drying huts.
Time to send someone on ahead to hire
The amazing Eagle Finders.
It is a time for them to make their way here
To us near the end of Deer Season.
They must come singing softly as they travel here,
Singing some go-to-sleep lullabies to the snakes.
Time for us to gather sourwood
From the Lily of the Valley Trees.
Time for us to build those small huts of sourwood
In our village.
Time for us to make small stakes of sourwood
To give to the Eagle killer.
Time for us to hum softly.
Time for the brave Eagle Finders come slowly
Along the trail to us, The Deer Clan.
Time for the Eagle Finders to lead the Eagle Killer to us,
Their cousins waiting by our river.

Golden Egle in Flight

Once in Silence
We Went Where Eagles Rest

Once in silence we greeted our brave cousins,
The Eagle Finders, with sign language.
We now again greet them.
We make them welcome in our village.
We show them the small house,
A small hut near our homes,
Newly built and big enough
For two or three of us to stand in,
And wide enough to spread the wings of eagles.
It is our new hut for drying eagle feathers.
Most of the village keeps on talking about everyday things.

73

Under a Sunflower Moon

No one speaks aloud about our Deer Kills,
Or about our need for Golden Eagle feathers.
We don't want the eagle to hear,
To hear us and seek revenge.
On the floor of the hut, we spread out tobacco leaves.
Outside the hut we sprinkle corn pollen
All around the edges of the walls.
"Long ago, before we came to Oklahoma,"
Said Grandmother Trueshot,
"Two Deerslayers, Two Eagle Finders
And I would go into the mountains.
We looked for a ledge in the forest.
We looked for a good hiding place nearby.
In silence I prepared the hiding place
By spreading out tobacco leaves to sleep on.
The Eagle Finders hid with me.
The Deerslayers brought
A freshly killed dear to the ledge.
We helped place his face to the east
And his legs to the south.
It rested in easy, plain sight for the eye of any Eagle to see.
We all hid in bushes nearby to wait, to watch for Eagles
To come to their feast.
Silently we said blessings.
Silently we said prayers.
Silently, the Eagle Hunters prepared their bows and arrows.
We all take turns sleeping.
We pray we don't have nightmares
About Eagles coming to kill us.
We drink water only.
We don't talk.
We don't eat.
Sometimes we wait two or three days.
Finally, we hear the swoosh of Eagles.
Usually there are two
Because the Golden Eagles hunt in pairs.
They spread themselves over the slain deer.
Bows and arrows are ready,

74

Jackie Kraft

Waiting
For the kill.
Only certain Eagle Finders are allowed to kill.
Sometimes they fast for four days and
Then sing down the Eagles.
We like to stay in silence.
The arrows find their marks.
Silently, I watch until I am sure all is finished.
I leave the area.
I go down the mountainside.
I put my mind on the coming spring, on butterflies,
On sunflowers and roses.
On Rose Quartz crystals
Gathered at midnight.
I make my way back to the village.
I say out loud to all who come near me,
'Two little, tiny white birds died today.'
If any Eagle hears me, it will be tricked into thinking,
I mean two little Bob-Whites were killed.
Everyone knows without me saying in few days
The Deerslayers will spread out clean, tanned deer hide
On the mountain ledge
For our cousins to place feathers from the fresh kills.
Our cousins will take all the tail feathers from each Eagle.
They stake the small sourwood planks around the kills.
The planks keep out vermin.
We wait more.
Our cousins are ready to take the feathers.
Pluckers wrap all the tail feathers in Deer hides.
Then they will take the wing feathers to be wrapped in another hide.
The four men will return to our village carrying the bundles
And go straight to the feather hut.
No talking, just sign language.
They pray for forgiveness.
They silently say more blessings
As they come down the mountain.
I have fresh water and vinegar ready
For the Eagle Finders to bathe the feathers.

Under a Sunflower Moon

After the soaking and rinsing,
We spread the feathers out
In the hut on tobacco leaves to dry.
I give a feather offering prayer
By blowing tobacco smoke over the feathers.
The Medicine man from our tribe
And our own priest come.
In silence, we greet one another.
In silence, we pray.
If there be nightmares, the shaman will do special exorcism rituals.
We will have our evening dance of celebration.
We will have a feast of new Deer meat.
We will honor the Eagle Finders
With many gifts.
We will give the Eagle Killers many gifts.
Then we all will rest and be thankful.
In the morning, our cousins
Will start for their home.
We will give them more gifts to take for their return.
In silence, we thank them for their sacred help.
We send prayers in sign language
For safe travels
During this frosty winter day."
It was Grandmother Trueshot's honor to teach me,
But it was my honor, a little girl, to learn.

Rain Making

"Sometimes in Oklahoma we need rain. I know how to bring the rain." Grandmother Trueshot began. "I saw the Rainmakers dying one by one on the Trail of Sad Tears. So, I asked them, the dying Rainmakers, to teach me how to make it rain. They saw the need to teach me. They knew I could be a messenger. I learned a little from each one so I could teach out here if I survived. Here is what they taught me."

Be careful who you choose to teach.
They must be careful listeners.
They must love water.
They must love the sky and sky people.
They must love clouds and wind and rain.
They must not fear the thunder.
They must not hide from lightning.
It helps if they are young, like seven.
They must know our sacred animals and objects.
They must know our blessings and prayers.
The priests, the Shamans, and the Medicine men must approve
Of your choice whom to teach.
You are Deer Clan.
Deer Clan members are all messengers.
You can carry the knowledge of Rainmaking
All the way West
To share with a chosen one or two.
Before you choose a Rainmaker,
You must be one.
Start by simple drumming to match
The heartbeat of Mother Earth.
When your heart matches her heartbeat,
Go to the river to bathe.
Look for clear, shallow running water.
Fall in love with the water.
If there be a waterfall, go gently into it.
Become one with the water.
Think of our seven directions

Under a Sunflower Moon

And all the places water can be.
Become one with all the places water can be.
Think of all the joy rain brings to animals,
And plants and crops and flowers and trees.
Think of joy in the eyes of our tribal members
When rain comes in times of need.
Become one with joy.
Fall in love with joy.
Dry yourself with tobacco leaves.
Lay yourself down
On tobacco leaves.
Shelter yourself away from others as you rest.
Now begins the important part.
Clear your mind.
Sit up crossed legged
Facing where the rain comes from,
Either Southwest or Northwest,
But mainly Southwest.
The best snow comes from the Northwest.
The best rain comes from the Southwest.
Be relaxed as your breath matches your heartbeat.
Match Mother Earth's heartbeat.
Send your mind from your body as far into the sky as it can go.
You will feel a bump on your head
When it reaches a ceiling in the heavens.
Really, you will.
With all your strength make your mind go fast
Either to the Southwest or the Northwest
As far as it can.
You will feel it bump again this time into rain
When it gets where it needs to go.
Really, it does happen.
In silence, let your heart begin to sing to the rain.
"Gentle rain, life giving rain,
Sacred blessing to us all,
Come now with me to my home,
To my people,
Thirsty for you

Jackie Kraft

Here in Oklahoma.
Come with me.
Let me bring you, the rain.
Let me, with you, ride on gentle clouds.
Let me fly, with you, on gentle winds.
Let me see your mighty lightning.
Let me hear your booming thunder.
Let me feel your many raindrops
Falling on my face.
Let me feel your fresh new water
Running through my hair.
Come along now with me
To my new dry and hungry homeland.
Come, be a gift of life.
Let me say out loud
My grateful thank-you's
As I dance in all your puddles.
Let me run with you to streamlets,
Let me swim into your rivers.
Let me gather you in buckets.
Please, let me be the same as you, good rain,
To all who want it now,
To all who need it now.
Let me bring the precious rain."

Monarch Butterfly

Rose Quartz Harvest

Once I knew where to harvest rose quartz
From the ground near the Valley of the Vapors.
Once I watched
The swan and the buffalo
Gather near the raccoons as they looked
In the starlight for food.
I saw the Panther stay gentle in the branch of a tree.
I saw Eagles soar above in the morning sun.
Beneath them lay abundance from the Creator.
Once I knew how to gather swan feathers
For the Shamen of our tribe.
Once I knew how to rest and be thankful
For all that is easy to come my way.
I bathed in the healing springs beside two Hopi men.
I traded red corn kernels and bears' claws
For Blue Corn still on a cob.

Jackie Kraft

The braves said they will return
To their home in the west
To watch for the Blue Kachina to return.
She will dance in their main square
And remove her mask.
They asked if my rose quartz was magic.
I replied, "I put my faith in my creator,
Who gave everyone and everything
A spark of herself.
I carry rose quartz to remind me
Of the spark of Manatowa Love
In everything and everyone."
They asked, "Could you share with us
Where you harvest rose quartz crystal
That we may take some pieces home?"
I said, "I pray, hunt and harvest at midnight
Beneath a sunflower moon.
But at sunset I sit on the side of the river.
I remember the stories I have heard,
And all the prayers I have heard.
I remember the maiden.
Who wore robes the color of the sunset.
I remember how she sat upon the river banks
Watching silver vapors in the mists.
She left her robes on the riverbanks.
She swam away with swans.
Manatowa covered her robes for her and
Turned them to rock crystals.
Yes, when we are healed,
I will show you where
I pray for spirit guidance.
I will help you with your rose quartz harvest.
I will show you how I harvest.
But can you tell me more about your Blue Kachina?
Can you tell me more of the Dog Star, Sirius?
Can you tell me more of your creation?
Can you tell me what you think of
Turquoise and butterflies?"

Swan Lake

CHAPTER 7

Uncle Scoot

Uncle Scoot was old widow Tiftley's brother. He was also my grandfather. One day he told a story to my cousins and me. We sat around the garden table in the shade.

"When I was a little boy, my mother sent me to a Catholic school. She didn't know any better. They tried to beat the Cherokee out of me. They told her, the Bible told them to. That it was all right to beat a child. 'Spare the rod and spoil the child.' Beating me every day did not work. I cried a lot, and one day I ran away. I hid in a building near town. I was so cold and hungry. A man was there.

"He found me still sobbing under his desk. He took his striped shawl off his shoulders. He kissed the hem, and then he wiped my tears with it. It was midnight.

"He gave me Matzah to eat. It was a giant cracker, but it tasted like heaven."

The man said, "I was beaten, too, but not as a child. My name is Jacob Pincus. We lived beyond the Pale in Russia. I was a grown man on a farm outside of Kiev, near Odessa, when soldiers beat me. They said I had gold. There was a pogrom, a killing of Jews. Not only was I a farmer, but I was also a teacher. The only gold I had was knowledge. In my language the word for teacher is rabbi. I am a rabbi in this building. What is the name for teacher in your language?"

I said, "*Dideyohvsgi*. God made me a Cherokee. I am not wrong to be Cherokee."

Jacob Pincus said, "From your lips to God's ears. Here, have some more Matzah. Have a little grape juice, too. I want to tell you a story. Have you ever seen a shepherd with his flock of sheep? He is very tender with all of them. Each one is precious and valuable. Sometimes he must move them along to new pasture.

"They stray off the path or get lost in the brambles. But he doesn't beat them with his staff. He would never hit or hurt the little lambs. He uses the best end of the rod that has the crook to gently pull each stray back on the path. 'Spare the Rod and Spoil the Child' is what you hear bible readers say. They are wrong.

"The phrase means don't forget to teach the child where he is supposed to go. Bring him gently back to the right path. Give him guidance with his life, or it will cause him ruin."

I started to sob again.

"That passage," said the softly spoken rabbi, is in the Bible in a language I know how to read. Hebrew. People, who beat others in the name of God, don't know Hebrew. They don't know the true meaning of the bible's words. The words were written by a wise Shepherd who grew up to be King David in a land of Milk and Honey. He knew how to treat little lambs.

"When you grow up, you can be as a shepherd. You can be a friend. You can be a teacher. You can be a Cherokee. Tell others the real meaning of that passage King David wrote. No one should ever be beaten."

My grandfather stood up. "That teacher, the Rabbi, knew my mother. Her family knew sadness because they walked the cold trail of frozen cries and tears all the way here to our Oklahoma reservation. That Rabbi, that teacher, took me home to her. They became even better friends. He became my new teacher.

"It was midnight when he found me. I sobbed my heart out under his desk wrapped in his prayer shawl, but I learned that I am valuable and precious in God's eyes just as you are. I scooted as far back into the darkness as I could under his desk and sobbed."

"Come out, you little scooter," he said kindly.

"I learned that day there may be evil in the world, but there is also kindness. I can pass the kindness on to others. I held hands with Sadness. She walked with me a long way. She led me to a place of where I could hold hands with someone new called Happiness. Silence was our prayer. We became as one. I am Cherokee." Uncle Scoot took a sip of his coffee and sighed.

"Let's have some crackers, Sally, and grape juice. Help me pass it out," said Mrs. Tiftley. We sat at the table together in thoughtful silence. All we cousins ate crackers and drank grape juice.

"I'm an old man now, but I have learned that whoever you need to meet next, you will meet. Whatever life lesson your soul needs to learn, you will be given the opportunity to learn it. Whatever the Universe wants to show you, it will find a way.

"The Creator is a compassionate being. Everything is provided for us. The land gives us food and medicines."

Uncle Scoot's voice was strong, "Native traditional ways are my path. I can live fully Cherokee in those ways. Silence is my only prayer."

Sequoyah and the Invention of the Cherokee Alphabet

CHAPTER 8

Sally's Poems

Blue Corn Harvest 7/08/14

I am a child of the Blue Corn Harvest.
I gather my magic under a Sunflower Moon.
In my medicine bag are seven Blue Corn Kernels,
Treasures saved last summer from a dying plant.
Sweet brittle mother, she whispered on the wind
Her truth to my heart.
I named all her Blue Corn children.
The first one I named Big Hope.
The next, I called Pure Blue Joy.
I named Long Sorrow, Reconciliation, No Waiting,
And Endless Harvest.
The last seed child I named True Love of Life.
Tonight, I will plant them, all seven, in red mud
By the riverbank in Eastern Oklahoma,
By the River of No Return,
Where the sweet potatoes bloom
Under my own Cherokee Sunflower Moon.
I will water the Blue Corn seeds while I dance
With my tears of good memories of you.
As I dance I will sing the whole night long
Of a whispered truth
Blue Corn Mother taught me.
I will sing to all the stars
And howl her wisdom to the morning sun.
If Long Sorrow blooms first,
I'll pick her blossoms and scatter them
To the frosty North wind.
If Reconciliation grows, I'll grind some corn seeds
To feed all my tribe.
I'll save seed children of Reconciliation

Jackie Kraft

To plant again
Under a Sunflower Moon.
When Big Hope, Pure Blue Joy,
No Waiting, Endless Harvest
And True Love of Life sprout at last,
My tribe will hold a Stomp,
And share the harvest
At the Pow Wow.
We will give thanks
To that Whispering Blue Corn Mother
For her blessings and for her endless truth of optimism.
Then, I will braid my hair with wild onions,
Paint my face with red mud,
Dance again with the fireflies
Under a Sunflower Moon.
I will lie down at last among the sweet potato vines,
And wait for you
My brave warrior,
To find me in the magic shadows,
And call my Blue Corn medicine,
Oh, so good.

Blue Corn

Hidden Garden for Shy Deer

Deep in the White Oak woods
On the Reservation
Of my grandmother's farm
Near the Raccoon River
In a secret clearing
I made a new garden for shy deer.
I am called Humble Bug.
I went before the dawn
To bless the stillness
Of the woods and the quiet
That my shy deer love.
I honored the fierce raccoon
For making a home nearby my garden,
And for being friendly to my shy deer.
I honor the turtles.
They are the favorite food of the raccoons.
I thank the turtles and the raccoons
Who will help make my garden
A haven of peace and plenty.
I wear pig lard on the bottom of my feet.
It frightens snakes away.
They think wild hogs are nearby
And coming to root them out
For a meal.
As the birds began to sing
I chant a blessing
To the East and to the West
Where the sun and the moon reside,
To the North and the South, the home
Of gentle winds and helpful rains.
I chant thanks to the double rainbow
That comes special to Cherokee after a rain.
I bless the earth that will nourish
All the seeds growing into
The best, favorite plants for my shy deer.

Here's what I plant:
Some clover, some alfalfa,
And Golden Rod for late August food,
Two apple trees, for food in the fall,
And a Plum Thicket.
The three Cherokee sisters,
Who are squash, corn and beans.
I planted one new White Oak tree,
The sacred guardian in the center
Of the clearing,
And I make a border of sunflowers
Around our secret garden.
Some Bloodroot medicine for me
We call Gi Tli U Wa Ta Li.
I plant one willow tree for winter food.
Then, in the cold, dark days of snow,
When only the tips of the branches,
Are tender for shy deer to eat,
When only the acorns are still plentiful
To find and feed on,
I will wait and watch
For my hungry friends to come.
I will say a blessing for them
That they may live in harmony with my clan
And all the creatures of the earth.
In the spring during
The peaceful dawn
And the quiet dusk,
I will call forth new rains and
The double rainbow
For the shy deer to admire.
Then all the shy deer will come
With little fawns to feed and
To thank the Humble Bug girl
For the feast of foods they love,
For the beauty,
For the love I, the shy girl,
The Humble Bug, bring to them.

Apple Trees

October Day

Yesterday geese flew south in form,
Sunlight glinting on wings so warm.
They left their homes all over town
Before the rain and leaves fell down.
I turned the furnace on today.
My dog looked up as if to say,
"It's not that cold.
You're feeling creaky and rather old."
It's time to find the rake,
Clean my yard, for neighbors' sake.
I sighed, resigned to my fate.
A day of hard work just won't wait.
Still, I wished for endless spring
And hoped I'd hear the robin sing.
Big piles of yellow, red, and brown

Jackie Kraft

Scattered leaves brought such a frown.
I paused to think nearby the shed
While late-start geese flew overhead
In earnest V-shapes, flapping hard
Through swirling smoke above my yard.
Spring will come again, I know,
It's guaranteed on Earth below.
If I could go with bird or leaf,
Then would I feel this simple grief
For mindless days that pass me by?
I'd float away; perhaps I'd fly
To where there's faith in things unseen,
Where skies are blue
And yards stay clean.

Cousins Janet & Sally playing dress up
with Grandma Cora's clothes

Jackie Kraft

Our Willow Tree

Gathering Corn Pollen
For My Medicine Bag

It must be at dawn,
Or even better about an hour before dawn
Just as the birds begin to sing.
They sing to wake us up and remind us
To either gather corn pollen,
Or tobacco leaves for our medicine bundles.
I gather my corn pollen in moonlight.
It goes into small, soft deerskin bags
That I tie carefully with sinews.
Four small bags are enough.
A little goes a long way.
But first, before I put my harvest in the bag,
I spread out four, fine big tobacco leaves.

Under a Sunflower Moon

Over them I sprinkle my new corn pollen to dry.
Gently, as the pollen dries, I stir pollen
With my Golden Eagle feather.
Once dried, I fold each tobacco leaf four times.
One time for the Good Father, South Wind.
One time for the Whispering Grandmother, East Wind.
One time for my Cold Uncle, North Wind.
And one time for the dear Old Mother, West Wind.
Then I stop.
In silence my heart chants three prayers.
One prayer for the Blue Dog Star in the heavens.
May she come soon to dance in the square
For our Hopi Friends in the West.
One prayer for the deep center heart of a healthy earth
And the generous harmony that can reach everyone.
Finally, one prayer for the center place
Where I stand in my garden
That I may live in peace and harmony with all
Plants and animals,
That I may continue to grow
Squash, Beans, Corn, Tobacco, and Sunflowers
On this beautiful earth in my Garden for the Shy Deer,
And that I can continue each year to gather corn pollen.
Now, deep into my medicine bundle
I place my four tobacco bundles in their little bags.
Gently, I blow my Cherokee breath,
All smokey,
With all my other prayers down into the bundle.
I have strong medicine to share.
I will stand firm, confident, humble and alert
For those in need.
I will wait for love, truth and kindness
To return to powerful rulers.
I will wait all day and continue my prayers
Until I can share my corn pollen
And dance under the next coming Sunflower Moon.

Jackie Kraft

Tobacco Plants in Spring Bloom

Sweet Smell of Tobacco

Not everyone is allowed today to grow tobacco.
Long ago it was cultivated and used for many purposes.
In the beginning it grew where rabbits dropped the seeds.
To find a plant of tobacco was a great and wonderful omen.
In our garden we pick some small leaves
And leave the rest to keep growing.
We make shallow pits to create tobacco smoke.
First, we blessed the pit,
And next we dry the leaves
Then, we blessed the tobacco leaves,
When they are completely dry,

95

Under a Sunflower Moon

We light a fire under them.
Then, we sprinkle pure river water
Over the burning leaves to create smoke.
Over the pit we stand stakes of White Oak
Soaked in clear, clean river water.
Around the stakes we drape hides of deer skin to dry.
The sweet smell of tobacco smoke
Makes the deer hide smell so good.
It helps tan the leather
And make it soft.
We are Deer Clan.
We use hide for many things.
Later we take the wet, burned leaves
To sprinkle outside
Around our homes.
It keeps the snakes away.

Chief John Ross' Cabin

Deer Season: How to Tan Hide

Find a friend who knows the old ways.
Say the old prayers and blessings for the deer.
Gather the materials you will need:
One oak barrel, two buckets of fresh, clear water,
Two buckets of fresh homemade apple vinegar.
Two pounds of salt,
One iron cauldron to make brain, liver, and fat soup.
Get scrapers, knives, and clean rags.
Make one fire pit for the oil tanning soup
Of brain, liver, and fat.
Make a smaller fire and the smoke pit for the tobacco.
Assemble a rack to dry the meat in a small hut.
(Nowadays, if you have a freezer you can ziplock
Pieces of deer meat and store immediately.)
Make a special place in the hut

For antlers and hooves to be stored.
When the Deerslayers bring the kill
In the very early morning or at sunset,
Have them hang it head up
From a tree limb in the shade.
Have everyone chant the prayers
And more blessings for the kill.
If it is a swift kill,
Gut immediately.
Skin quickly.
Let the meat cool.
Make the oil tanning soup in the cauldron.
Put the water, vinegar and deer hide to soak
 24 hours in the oak barrel.
Drain, salt, scrape off hair. Repeat.
Drape the hide to dry over a large rock.
Make the tobacco fire and start the smoke.
Drape the hide over the pit
On oak branches soaked in water.
Turn over to do both sides.
Rest and be thankful.

TAH-CHEE
A CHEROKEE CHIEF
Philadelphia Published by E.C Biddle

More Than the Sum

I am more than the sum of my ancestors.
Yes, I am mixed breed.
I am an unregistered Cherokee.
Hear, Oh Israel,
I am more than all the prayers of my ancestors.
Between the mezuzah and the spice box
Is my mongrel soul.
A soul is like my medicine bundle
Containing all the memories
I value in my ancestors.
It's full of love, strength, forgiveness, and questions.
I search within for my Cherokee soul
Bundled up with my Huegenaut,
Quaker Christian soul
Bound up with my red-neck southern,

Under a Sunflower Moon

Slave owner-planters souls from
Mississippi, Louisiana, Tennessee, and Virginia.
Wrapped inside my Oklahoma red dirt, battered soul,
Tied up with my Swiss, Basque, Scottish,
Irish, Welch, German, French,
Ashkenazi Jewish souls, and
The souls who also walked the Trail of Frozen Tears,
But stopped at the Arkansas - Missouri State line.
I am more than the sum of all who went before me,
All who had hope and despair.
All who had laughter and bitter tears of disappointment,
All who watched the sunrise
And prayed each day for better times.
I want to fit in with all my heritage,
But I must fit in with today.
Could I start my own clan?
If I could,
I will call it the clan of the Sunflowers,
They will be friends of the deer
And the long-hair clans.
They may carry O-negative blood
In their positive hearts.
My clan roots will grow deep in red dust.
They shall drink in red water from red mud
Made by recycled tears that all the ancestors once shed.
As the German poet Goethe once recommended,
I will "turn my face to the sun."
He said, if I do, I will not notice the shadows.
But I do want to remember
The darkness of the shadows,
And write my own stories
About Trickster Rabbits
Who reincarnate as politicians.
I also want to be a guiding force for good in the world.
Like the great chiefs of all the indigenous people,
Like the great charitable
Influencers of civilizations,
Like the great rabbis who taught those souls

Jackie Kraft

(Who knew no bible verses by heart)
To recite the alphabet in Hebrew as they waited in line
To be gassed in the ovens,
(Because God invented the Alphabet
And he hears even whispers in his own language
And knows what you mean
As you recite the Alphabet
If that is all you know in Hebrew.)
Like the great Martin Luther King whose
Dying words forgave all those who persecuted him.
Besides, I would rather count coup than take scalps.
I would rather dance among the flowers
Who turn their faces to the sun.
I want to search for the truth.
My clan flag will be the color of the blue sky of summer
In Oklahoma when July is in my garden.
I will fly my flag proudly in the garden
I made for the shy deer.
The design in the blue cloth will show the Pleides above.
The sunflowers growing below.
What you won't see;
What you cannot see,
Are all the invisible bears
Who will hunt me down and call me Leah.
(A Hebrew name for Sadness.)
If ever I leave my peaceful garden,
Or let unkindness enter my heart in our sanctuary,
Or if I ever forget to thank God
For my unregistered,
Mongrel Cherokee soul.

Flag

Brave Warrior

Brave Warrior of the noonday sun.
Gentle lover of the night.
You play with laughing winds and silly flowers.
Find me now.
I sleep with the leaves of squash blossoms
And curling beans.
I weave sweet potato vines and tobacco for our bed.
I braid my hair with red rose petals and yellow ribbons.
I listen to the Raccoon River
Slowly moving over rocks nearby.
I watch the heart-shaped leaves
Of the sunchokes call your name in the breeze.
I watch always for you in the sunset.
Find me now
In the starlight,
In the shadows
Under the Sunflower moon.

Jackie Kraft

When Adam Braided Eve's Hair

When Adam braided Eve's hair,
He used a rose of 13 petals fair
With centered stamens, numbered five.
He said, "Sit here, my dear,
And wait for sunlight to arrive.
Feel free to dream
Beside this little garden stream.
The days ahead are ours to hold.
Remember all that we've been told."
Eve sniffed a pomegranate,
"What you say,
Then so it is,
But for today,
I want to be
Where apples lay."
Beside the knowledge
Of this tree.

Gift of the Spider

If a spider comes into your life,
You should feel blessed.
Celebrate the spider
And her gift of weaving
With understanding eyes.
Do not kill her.
Just delicately escort her outside

Jackie Kraft

And wish her well.
She's fierce in her expectations
And fearless in her resolve.
She is reclusive, productive, opportunistic,
Small and creative.
With simple needs she is the center
Of her own universe.
She weaves one magnificent web after another.
She works alone
Flinging endless silk threads to the heavens.
She makes one delicate web after another
Like an artist with a perfect eye for painting beauty,
Like a poet making rhythm from her mind
And bringing forth a lovely rhyme,
With endless words that flow
And make a poem turn out right,
Like a writer spinning an infinity of stories
To ensnare an unsuspecting reader,
Like the thoughts that once written string together
Across a page of prose,
Like the phrases of wonder, hope, and despair,
Woven in order from tender start to strong finish,
Like a storyteller placing
A careful arrangement of each word,
Like an editor who carefully considers flow,
She continues a plan for her audience
Doubling back to bring forth the magic,
Wonder, whimsy, suspense, and joyous cunning
Into her own masterpiece,
To the very last powerful sentence of a new creation.
The gift of the spider's web is on display for those writers,
Needing a totem for inspiration, to observe and
To appreciate all the raw, intricate beauty
Of her endless designs.
The spider is like a tireless composer
Making a melody from nothing
Into a full symphony from wisdom within,
And she, neither helpless, nor hopeless.

Under a Sunflower Moon

She can toil between sidewalk cracks
And a marble façade to make a work
So perfect that when finished,
Is one astonishing surprise.
She is a totem for writers
Who have eyes to see
And the wisdom to appreciate
Creating something from little or nothing
To display.
And then, just as a performer
On opening night,
She will huddle humbly, disguising her pride,
In the very center of her web
And wait
To surprise and ensnare
An unsuspecting audience
Full of admiration.

Paul 4/2015

To be in a Universe
Where at least one planet has
A spring of wildly blooming flowers
Would have been enough,
But I was granted something better
By a thoughtful God,
An older brother.
An older brother was the precious gift
I least expected,
But like a silent and glorious sunrise that
No one notices at first,
Paul became a part of my daily routine,
Something to depend upon.
I'm glad I found you, Paul Ryan.
We thought we were cousins.
You, more than I, look more like our mother.
A beauty in her own time.
You have her black curly hair and widow's peak,
Her very deep blue eyes, her rosy cheeks, her brilliant smile,

Her sense of humor, and her amazing laugh.
You were both in full bloom at death.
Like spring our mom slipped away,
And then silently without notice you did, too.
While the world went to sleep,
Under a blanket the winter snow,
I was left behind to contemplate
A generous God,
Who let me know you
For a small bit of time.
How lucky we all were
To have known you.
How happy I was to be a younger sister.
I wanted to hang on to you
The same way I gather roses
And hold them close in spring.
Instead, I watch for cold snow and
Wish a lovely Universe were not so cruel.
Paul, where did your hopeful soul go?
Will we truly meet again as promised?
Will we meet again
In a kinder heaven?
I wait, I hope, for it to be.

Jackie Kraft

Dance

Let us dance among the roses
Beneath a restless moon.
I'll never speak of heartaches.
I'll sing a gentle tune.
Please hum along in stardust
Sprinkled like the rain
And drink in silver moonbeams.
It takes away the pain.
The sun exists with shadow.
We have known it all along.
Love everything that happens,
The good times and the bad.
It's all a part of living,
The ups, the downs, the sad.
Each life has special meaning.

Under a Sunflower Moon

The truth is what we seek.
We pray for easy passage
Both the mighty and the meek.
It helps to dance in roses
And sing a hopeful tune.
Let us treasure one another.
Flower season ends too soon.

Belonging

I belong to the universe.
I am a child of God.
I make my own way.
I am who I am.
I tell myself I am Cherokee
Of the Deer Clan.
Who cares if I am registered with the tribe?
I know who I am.
I am the Double Rainbow Girl
The little humble Humbug Girl.
I descend from Many Stars
Who was buried along
The western trails of falling tears.
I am a descendant of her daughter
Humble Bug,
Who, she, as a child, carried
The Medicine Bundle
Of our very sacred things.
Her teacher was Grandma Trueshot, a Star Woman.
She was the grandmother of Mrs. Tiftley,
Also, a Star Woman,
A messenger
And my teacher.
She was grandmother
Of my grandfather,
Uncle Scoot.
I am descendent of Humble Bug
Sometimes my teachers called me HumBug's Memory.
My name is *Tsalgi,* Sally.
I watch the stars
As I dance
Under Sunflower Moon.

On the Reservation

Turtle Wisdom

Go Slow.
Look at things up close.
Be cautious.
Follow your own path.
Be humble.
Be an example of peace.
Resting is good.
Withdraw inside your shell
If it is important to think alone,
Your Spirit Guide will find you
In the quiet.
Meditate.
Not everyone can be an eagle.
Enjoy your own journey.
Let the peace of the reservation
Embrace you on your journey.

Jackie Kraft

Here's why: Every turtle has a purpose
And every turtle knows survival.
It's best to keep your head down,
Your eye on the facts before you.
Curl up when you need to.
Smell the Roses.

Downstream from Politics

If you made a promise,
Keep it.
If you broke a promise,
Apologize and fix it.
If you helped someone,
Pat yourself on the back.
If you hurt someone,
Make amends.
If you found gold on tribal lands,
Give it back.
If you broke a treaty, fix it.
If you stole land from Cherokee,
Make restitution.
If you dug up indigenous burial mounds,
Give all the bones and artifacts back.
If you registered some Cherokee,
But left out other Real People,
Why were you so selfish?
Quit messing around.
Don't be a turkey.

Forgive Me, as I Forgive Others

(Sin, such a great Greek word
For the phrase 'miss the mark.')
I forgive everyone for everything,
Past, present, and future.
For things seen and unseen,
For things said and unsaid,
For things heard and not heard,
For things done and not done.
I forgive the mistakes I made,
I forgive myself for all I the things
I should have done,
For kindness I should have shown to others,
But never did show,
For unconditional love I should have given,
But somehow selfishly withheld.
I forgive everyone, for everything
Including myself.
We all sin. We are all sinners.
"For it is in forgiving
That we are forgiven."

The Clan of the Sunflower, the Humble Ladybug, and the Moon

May I tell you of a special day Grandmother Trueshot
Got up one morning to greet the sun?
It was the year 1867.
It was the season of marigolds and ladybugs.
It was the night of the full Sunflower Moon.
She was in her garden with most of her children,
Grandchildren, cousins, brothers, sisters
And nieces, nephews, friends, neighbors,
Shamans, medicine men, and priests.
The Deerslayers in our clan
And their cousins, the Eagle Finders, came.
All looked to the Eastern Sky.
The deer came to feed.
The Red-Tail Hawk circled in the morning sky
The young Rainmakers were there, too.
They all watched the sunrise.
Some grandchildren brought Grandmother a blanket
To warm her shoulders.

Jackie Kraft

Some brought their rattles and drums.
Some brought corn pollen and Eagle feathers.
She greeted them and said,
"Thank you all for coming.
It's been a good life.
You can see I'm getting very old.
I feel it's time to die.
Can you lift me up in joy?
Can you help me dance
One more time
Beneath a Sunflower Moon?
Can you hold me upright
And move me around the circle?
When it's time to go to heaven.
Can you place me on my mound?
Can you make my face look Eastward
To watch the morning sun?
Please, don't close my eyelids.
Lay me down on Tobacco, Cedar, Sage and Sweetgrass.
Please sprinkle me with Corn pollen
And beans, squash, and corn.
Plant a white oak in my garden,
And a willow tree nearby.
Think how they both love raindrops
And think that so do I.
Remember all that's sacred.
Let me die a gentle peace
Here among my sunchokes,
My bugs and moonbeams, too.
Once my soul has gone to heaven
Dance around me one more time tomorrow
Beneath a Sunflower moon.
Don't moan for me in sorrow.
Please chant a happy tune.
My soul will be in Heaven.
I'll be free to rest there soon.
I've loved that I was human,
And a messenger to boot,

Under a Sunflower Moon

I could have been a rock, a tree,
Or just some simple dirt.
I was glad to be a person
And learn all what I could be.
I was glad to be a teacher.
With all the world to see.
I may have walked the frozen trail,
But I'm content enough to be
And have all the joy in a lifetime
Of good things meant for me.
Just kiss my cheeks goodbye.
Do not mourn me with your tears.
Just remember all I've taught you
Throughout the future years.
Let me travel on without you.
Let my soul soar to the stars.
I'll watch you with our sky people.
Perhaps we'll wait for you on Mars.
Wear your feathers to remember.
Wave your flag in peaceful ways.
Let your hearts embrace the good times.
Sing and dance your heartfelt feelings.
The good lord loves us one and all,
So, spend your lifetime singing
What you know to be so true.
Ring around me with your dancing.
Help others pick an honest Chief.
Think kindly as you grieve.
Bury me by Sunflowers
Don't mark my grave at all.
I'm just an old time, humble woman
Who tried to do her best.
Could you plant one bean, one corn, one squash
Upon my gentle breast?
I pray their roots will wake my soul
Next spring from all my winter rest.
When September comes a year from now,
After harvest's come and gone,

118

Jackie Kraft

Please remember me with love.
The evening moon will come up slowly.
Please howl, and dance and stomp
Beneath my Sunflower moon.

A Sunflower Moon

Appendix 1

Vocabulary

AGALI	Sunshine
ANI GATO GEW	Wild Potato Clan
ANI GILOHI	Long-Hair or Twister Clan
ANI KAWA	Deer Clan
ANI KUTAN	Priest Clan
ANI SAHANI	Blue Holly Clan
ANI TSISKWA	Bird Clan
ANI WAYA	Wolf Clan
ANI WODI	Paint Clan
Ani No Qui S	star
Ani Si D	place to lay down
Awi	Deer
Awa Hili	Eagle
OSIYO	Hello
KITAWAH	An original town near the Tuskasegee River; one of the seven mother towns
Ka No Na	corn beater
TIS A GWA	Northern Bob White
TSALAGI, ANA Yun WIYA	Cherokee name or themselves; Real people or principal people
ANI GA DU WAGI	Real people or Kituwah people
TUSKAEGEE RIVER	turtle place; crawling turtle
SHAY RO KI; CHEY RO TI CO WI	principal people, real people
JISTU	a rabbit
NUN N EHI	friendly spirit, a traveler, sometimes invisible, sometimes a visible human
U NET LA NV I	Greatest Spirit, Creator, God
U NV QUO LA DA	Rainbow
Yunwi Tsunsdi or Yunwi Tsunsdi Gah	Little People, E.T.
YVWI US DI	Little person, dwarf, fairy, E.T.,

	invisible spirit
CADDO	*a tribe from homelands of what is today Arkansas, Louisiana, Texas, and Oklahoma.*
QUAPAW	*sometimes called Akansa, they were removed from their homeland in 1834. Their language is like Osage, Ponca, and Omaha.*
OSAGE	*A tribe whose members mostly live in Oklahoma now. Some were cheated. Also called A Na Sa Si*

Si Lu	*Corn*
Nv Do	*Moon*
Nv Do Di Se S Di	*Moon Counter*
Guvi Sgu Wi	*little white birds*
Ka La Gi Sa	*Swan*
TSA RO GI	*Cave People*
U Ni Li Si	*Grandmother of a group of children*
Nv Wo Ti	*medicine*
Gi Tli U Wa Ta Li	*Bloodroot*
Da Lo Ni Gei	*gold*

Appendix 2

Historical Timeline, Treaties

30,000-35,000 years ago	Ancestors of what are now called Native American tribes crossed the land bridge from Asia to North America.
8000-10,000 years ago	Native Americans spread into what is now called south eastern United States.
1541 A.D.	Hernando de Sota, Spanish conqueror, was the first to lead a European expedition into what is now Arkansas. He wanted gold and the Fountain of Youth. He crossed the Mississippi River south of what is now Memphis. The tribes living at the time in the area were Quapaw, Caddo, Osage, as well as the (later called) Five Civilized Tribes – the Cherokee, Creek, Choctaw, Chickasaw and the Seminole.
1673 A.D.	Father Jacques Marquette and Louis Joliet, Frenchmen, traveled down the Mississippi River as far south as what is now called the Arkansas River. They went back to Canada.
1682 A.D.	La Salle, a French explorer, claimed what was later named the Mississippi and tributaries and bay area for France. He named the area Louisiana for his King, Louis XIV. The Algonquian and the Chippewa are credited with the two native words, *Missi Sippi*, meaning flowing large water. The French called it the Colbert River, then the St. Lawrence River.
1686 A.D.	Henri de Tonti, Italian-born French Military officer, claimed what is now Arkansas for France. He lost one hand and wore a hook in its place. He built a small trading post that was the first permanent

	European settlement in the new world. He established a relationship with the Quapaw Tribe.
1768 A.D.	Treaty of Hard Labor
1770 A.D.	Treaty of Lochaber
1772 A.D.	Jean-Baptiste Bernard de la Harpe, a French explorer noticed a stone outcrop on what became called the Arkansas River. The formation was later named Little Rock, Arkansas
1785 A.D.	November Treaty of Hopewell
1786 A.D.	January Treaty of Hopewell
1798 A.D.	Treaty of Tellico
1791 A.D.	Treaty of Philadelphia
1785 A.D.	Treaty of Holstons
1803 A.D.	The Louisiana Purchase
1804-5 A.D.	The Hunter/Dunbar Expedition in which President Thomas Jefferson sent a secret group to explore what is now called Arkansas.
1824 A.D.	Fort Gibson established
1828 A.D.	The first Printing of the *Cherokee Phoenix* newspaper was printed in both Cherokee and English.
1830 A.D.	President Andrew Jackson/congress passed the Indian Removal Act of Congress, May 28, 1830.
1831-1850 A.D.	Ethnic cleansing.
1832 A.D.	Andrew Jackson and Congress Valley of Vapours & the Hot Springs area Federal Reserve
1835 A.D.	The Treaty of the New *Echota*, Georgia, St. Louis River and the Mississippi (Great) River. The Treaty of Removal was not accepted by many Cherokees.
1835 A.D.	First groups going west on the Trail of Tears
1838-9 A.D.	Bitter Winter Trail of Tears

1851 A.D.	Treaty of Fort Laramie
1867 A.D.	United States Peace Commission
1876 A.D.	*Qualla* Boundary
1889 A.D.	April 22, 1889, First Oklahoma Land Run
1891 A.D.	September 22, 1891, Land Run
1892 A.D.	April 19, 1892, Land Run
1893 A.D.	September 16, 1892, Land Run
1895 A.D.	Distribution/Kickapoo Lands
1898-1914 A.D.	Dawes Rolls
1907 A.D.	Oklahoma Territory becomes a state
1940 A.D.	First law protecting Bald Eagles
1962 A.D.	The Protection Act was amended to include protection for the Golden Eagle.
1998 A.D.	First White House Conference / Economic Development Native American Indian Communities

Onions Drying

Appendix 3

Suggested Sources for More Information

Qualla Boundary

William "Will" Thomas Purchase

Trail of Tears

Iroquois History

Oconaluftee Indian Village, North Carolina

Cherokee Crafts

Oklahoma Indian Territory

Seven Mother Towns

Seven Clans of Cherokee

Modern Tribal Government of the Cherokee

Golden Eagle and the Red-tailed Hawk

President Ulysses S. Grant and Federal Indian Policy

The Hunter /Dunbar Forgotten Expedition to Arkansas

Clinton-Gore Policy and Native Americans

Sacred numbers to the Cherokee

Wilma Mankiller

Pvt. John G. Burnett and Cherokee Removal

Four sacred medicines of the Cherokee

1311 caves in North Carolina

Caddo Cave – The Place of Crying

About the Author

While in Kansas City, Jackie Kraft produced news, interviews, promos, and mini-documentaries for the CBS affiliates KCTV-5 and KCMO. She produced The Walt Bodine Show for KMBZ and was on-air talent, producing news, editorials, and interviews for The Women's Show at KCUR-PBS.

Jackie earned a B.S. and M.S. from Kansas University. She taught Special Education for Behavior Disorders, Autistic, and Learning Disabilities children in both Shawnee Mission and Olathe District Schools. She was a community volunteer, serving as an officer on many Boards of Directors. She now lives in Oklahoma.

www.underasunflowermoon.com

Acknowledgments

I would like to thank my children, Elizabeth and Brady, their children, Olivia, Jack, Ann, and Kenny, and my brothers, Paul Winterburg, and Mike Hawkins. In addition, I thank my many cousins for their steadfast love and encouragement. I thank my extended family of both my husbands, John Davis and Jacob Kraft. It gives me endless pleasure to remember all the good times I have had with my family.

To the alpha and beta readers, writing club members, book club members, and those who wrote reviews, I give my thanks. Your help and comments made a difference in the finished book.

My special thanks must go to Amy M. Le of Quill Hawk Publishing for questions, comments, helpful criticism, and editing. What a valuable service of care you gave me! Thank you also to Virginia Moffett for her artwork and guidance.

This book is based on memories of conversations with my relatives over the years of my life. Names, characters, incidents, and most places are from the author's imagination and are used fictitiously. Any resemblance to actual people, living or dead, is a coincidence. Some locations are historic but used fictiously.

May I tell you, dear reader, I still have the three corn necklaces I wear over my heart? But deep within my heart, I still remember Mrs. Tiftley's lessons of our brave Deer Clan, one of the seven Clans of the Cherokee, and all her stories. That time was 1950 near Tahlequah, Oklahoma.

I am a member of the Blue Corn Harvest, a friend of Red Dirt and Sunflower Moons. I am a spiritual friend of Mrs. Tiftley's grandmother, Elise Many Stars, and her Great-Grandmother Trueshot. Their friendly spirits still guide my voice and my footsteps. I thank them, the spirits of my own Grandmother Cora Maize and Mrs. Tiftley from the bottom of my corn necklace-covered heart.

Until we meet again, thank you,
Sally Jackie